Murderous Crossing

A Comic Agatha Christie Style
Interactive Mystery

by

David Landau

Music & Lyrics by

Nikki Stern

NEW YORK HOLLYWOOD LONDON TORONTO

SAMUELFRENCH.COM

No one shall commit or authorize any act or omission by which the copyright of, or the right to copyright, this play may be impaired.

No one shall make any changes in this play for the purpose of production.

Publication of this play does not imply availability for performance. Both amateurs and professionals considering a production are strongly advised in their own interests to apply to Samuel French, Inc., for written permission before starting rehearsals, advertising, or booking a theatre.

No part of this book may be reproduced, stored in a retrieval system, or transmitted in any form, by any means, now known or yet to be invented, including mechanical, electronic, photocopying, recording, videotaping, or otherwise, without the prior written permission of the publisher.

IMPORTANT BILLING AND CREDIT REQUIREMENTS

All producers of *MURDEROUS CROSSING must* give credit to the Author of the Play in all programs distributed in connection with performances of the Play, and in all instances in which the title of the Play appears for the purposes of advertising, publicizing or otherwise exploiting the Play and/or a production. The name of the Author *must* appear on a separate line on which no other name appears, immediately following the title and *must* appear in size of type not less than fifty percent of the size of the title type.

MURDEROUS CROSSING first opened at the Murder To Go Dinner Theatre in Cedar Knolls, NJ in January 1993 under the direction of David Landau. The cast was as follows;

MADAM HASTINGS/ISABELLA . . . . Michelle Palmier
DT. CLURROT/HOWARD . . . . Michael Mooney
NICOLE FOLLETTE . . . . Dawn Allyn
JOHN ROTHCHILD . . . . Michael Parker
VIVIAN ROTHCHILD . . . . Leslie Williams
LORD BENNET . . . . John Trapani

INTRODUCTION

I invented the interactive mystery play back in the early 1980s as an attempt to mix environmental theater with audience involvement. My goal was to allow the audience to experience the story as if they were extras in a movie. The entire production, from script to props, direction to surroundings, was oriented towards encompassing the audience in the world of the mystery and not merely with the game of solving it. Mystery parlor games existed since the turn of the century. As theater, it is the story of the characters which must always take center stage - a story of people who find themselves in desperate situations and are compelled to perform desperate acts. The comedy must come from the characters and not at their expense or that of the story.

It can become tempting for cast members to play for a laugh, but this seldom works. The audience laughs the most at things that are played straight - discovering the humor for themselves. Audiences identify and sympathize with characters that are real and seldom with caricatures. An actor's approach to an interactive mystery should be no different than that taken to Shakespeare or any other theatrical work. Why is the character there, what are they thinking, why are they doing what they do and what do they want? The more real, the more the audience becomes involved in this new reality and the more both they and the performers will enjoy the experience. The audience itself is utilized by the performer as a prop, a confidant, another cast member. The audience is on stage with them.

In a true mystery there can be only one logical culprit, pointed out not only by the clues, but by the motivation, personality and situation that character finds himself/herself in. While there are a number of other likely suspects, this character is the inevitable guilty party. The mystery has been sown well when the average of correct guesses is 10 - 20%. By the end of the play, when all is revealed, the audience should sigh a collective 'Of course, I should have thought of that!'

The interactive mystery play offers theater patrons, performers and producers many unique opportunities. The audience can be taken to the edge with suspense and then suddenly dropped into a humorous release of tension. The characters can become so real that they can reach out and touch the audience, literally. The theatrical fourth wall is placed behind the audience. If done correctly, the interactive play can be one of the most involving forms of theater possible.

David Landau

Creator of the first interactive mystery play, *The Mystery Express,*
Dec. 1982

Member of The Dramatists Guild and Mystery Writers of America

NOTES ON PRODUCTION

PERFORMANCE SPACE

The following play was designed to be performed in a dining room, dinner theater, night club, theater-in-the-round, or a thrust stage where the acting area is level with the first row. The intention is to make the audience feel like they are actually in the location of the story. The performance is a sort of reverse theater in the round, with action performed around the circumference of the seating area, as well as down the aisles and in the center. The audience should be seated at tables, either dinner or cocktail. Tables could be added in font of the first row in the case of thrust or arena stages. Audience members can also be seated on stage.

SCENES & BREAKS

The script is formatted into four or five scenes running in length from 12 to 20 minutes. Between each scene is time to serve a course of a meal, serve drinks, or play music as desired. During these breaks characters mingle helping to establish character and reveal information to the audience in a one on one manner. The script can easily be adapted to eliminate some of these breaks. If this is the desire, black-outs should take place between scenes, with an intermission between either scenes 2 and 3 (if four scenes) or 3 and 4 (if five scenes). There should be some kind of break just before the finale scene to allow audience members to hand in their guesses as to 'whodunit'.

MUSICAL NUMBERS

The musical numbers in the show have been designed to be performed to a taped play back. Once a performance license has been secured, an audio tape with recordings of both the instrumentals and the composer singing the lyrics can be obtained from Samuel French. Also on the tape is the opening theme music which is to be used at the beginning of each scene.

For more information contact Samuel French at info@samuelfrench. com.

Music & Lyrics were composed by Nikki Stern.

AWARDING PRIZES

The 'Sleuth Sheets' are handed out with the programs at the beginning of the night and collected by the characters before the finale scene. They should be handed to the stage manager, who will sort out the correct answers. After the curtain call, the correct answers are handed to the main character, who reads out the names of the successful sleuths. Generally, all correct answers are placed in a hat and a character draws one name. A prize is then awarded to that patron by a cast member. The prize can be a bottle of wine, a t-shirt, almost anything. It's the thought that counts.

CAST

FATHER CASSE-COU	The priest. He has a drinking habit.
CONTESSA NICOLE FOLLETTE	The bride. French.
LORD ARTHUR BENNET	The bride's friend. A wealthy British banker in London and the bride's ex-lover.
JONATHAN ROTHCHILD	The groom. Real name Stan Meyerhoff, an American actor.
VIVIAN ROTHCHILD	The groom's "sister." Real name Susan Starr, a bank robber from Oklahoma.
ISABELLA CORANOVA	Italian waitress, a gold digger run out of Monaco for immoral activities.
MISS HASTINGS	British, Ship's cruise director. (Same actress as **ISABELLA**)
HOWARD KREPPS	An out of work American actor, now a waiter on board.
INSPECTOR PIERRE CLURROT	French Luxembourg detective. (Same actor as **HOWARD**)

TIME

1923

PLACE

Dining room of the HMS VICTORIA, en route between Belgium and England. There is a head table at which are five chairs, five table settings and a wedding cake. Also present is a large steamer trunk.

The program cover will look like a wedding announcement.

> The HMS VICTORIA is proud to be the vessel of matrimony for the union of the Contessa Nicole Follette and John D. Rothchild during its crossing from Ostend, Belgium to Dover, England.

Inside the program is a sleuth sheet asking "Whodunit? Howdunit? & Whydunit?" and notes on how to play. "Welcome aboard the HMS Victoria. Leave your troubles at the door and embark with us on a journey across the English Channel and into the muddy waters of mystery and intrigue. As the story unfolds, we extend an invitation to you to participate and solve 'whodunit.'"

On each table are copies of The London Times Gazette.

> FOWLERS TO FOLD?
> The British Fowlers Company's troubles have worsened as customers have begun to shy away from medicines that contain arsenic as an active ingredient, thus slumping sales of the once popular

Fowlers Fever Solution. Many fear the company will claim bankruptcy. See page 3, Financials section.

LORD BENNET HELPS CONTESSA COURT LOVE

The real news is that our Lord Bennet, one of London's most powerful bankers, is on the continent helping to arrange the marriage of his close (some say intimate) friend the Contessa Follette. The lucky man is the simply yummy American, John Rothchild of the famously wealthy Rothchilds. This shouldn't matter too much to the Contessa, whose francs are in Lord Bennet's piggy, but at least it's nice for her to know she's not marrying beneath her. The bells will ring on board the small but luxurious HMS VICTORIA. We're not invited. But don't feel too sad, I'm sure we'll catch them honeymooning at the place they first met – the white cliffs of Dover. Just look for the couple eating escargot and french fries.

LUXEMBOURG LOSES MADMAN

Luxembourg police seem to have just missed nabbing the homicidal maniac who has evaded European officials for months and is believed responsible for the disappearance of international financier Gerard Shepard. The murderer, called The Marquis la Mort (The lord of death) by police, has gone under the names William Rasputan, Edward Ripper and Philip de Sade. He was tracked across the Belgium boarder, identified by a large steamer trunk with blood stains about the edges which he always had shipped with him.

FINANCIER MISSING

Gerhard J Shepard, the famed financier of London, seems to be missing – though many believe he is only hiding from his wife and creditors. See page 2, Financials section.

PRE-SHOW MINGLE

Miss Hastings, dressed in a white ship uniform and officer's cap will welcome guests aboard. They will be seated by her and Lord Bennet – who recognizes them as European aristocrats, and Vivian Rothchild – who thanks them for coming to her brothers wedding, and admires women's jewelry, inquiring on peoples net worth, etc.

Inspector Clurrot will be mingling, asking guests if they may have brought a large steamer trunk on board with them – one seems to have been found with no name on it. Also whether they are friends with or have seen Gerhard J Shepard, the wealthy financier.

Father will greet guests and ask them if they know how a wedding is supposed to go – he's only done funerals before.

Scene I

(Ship Horn blast. Lights up. **INSPECTOR CLURROT**
is looking over the trunk. **FATHER** *looks nervous and
downs a drink.* **MISS HASTINGS** *raises her glass. All
others are absent.)*

MISS HASTINGS. Ladies and Gentlemen? Ladies and Gentlemen, please allow me to introduce myself. I am your
cruise director Miss Hastings and now if you will all
raise your glasses with me as we set sail and toast with
me by saying Goodbye Belgium *(everyone repeats it)*
Hello England *(everyone repeats it).*

*(She downs her drink, which apparently was very strong,
then notices* **CLURROT** *at the steamer trunk.)*

MISS HASTINGS. Inspector Clurrot? What on earth are you
doing? We can't have someone's baggage in the dining
room!

CLURROT. I located this particular piece in the kitchen.
I suspect it is no ordinary luggage, Madam Hastings.
But the corpus delicti.

*(***CLURROT*** begins to swings open the trunk. Nothing
falls out.)*

MISS HASTINGS. No!

(As **CLURROT** *speaks he will pull out from the trunk a
bottle marked "Poison," a large knife, a wire and a gun,
placing them on top of the trunk.)*

CLURROT. Que. This is exactly what I have been looking
for. The steamer trunk of this Marquis de Morte, a
homicidal genius and master of deception. He could
be anyone. Some say, like Jack the Ripper, he leads a
double life. One of secure respectability and the other
of sinister scheming.

MISS HASTINGS. A virtual Jekyll and Hyde.

CLURROT. Exactament. My little grey cells tell me that this sudden rash of food poisoning among the crew is no accident. You did not partake of the shepherd's pie from the crew mess, no?

(**MISS HASTINGS** *picks up a bowl of mush.*)

MISS HASTINGS. Not yet. But the Shepard's pie is always so popular.

CLURROT. Perhaps if the crew was aware that the prime ingredient tonight was one Gerhard J Shepard, the missing wealthy financier, they would not have all had seconds.

(**CLURROT** *pulls a hand out of the trunk. They both look down at the bowl.* **CLURROT** *puts his finger in and pulls out a ring and slips it onto the hand.* **MISS HAST-INGS** *gives the bowl to a table of guests.*)

MISS HASTINGS. It's on the house.

FATHER. Should I prepare a funeral service?

CLURROT. Not yet, Father. I found the cook tied up with Monsieur Shepherd's clothing in the walk-in freezer in the crew kitchen. He was, how you say, out cold.

MISS HASTINGS. This is terrible. It's bad enough to have a homicidal maniac hiding aboard our ship, but on a specially chartered cruise for the Countess Nicole Follette's wedding – this just won't do.

CLURROT. Alas, Miss Hastings, I am afraid you have little to say in the matter. Your stowaway is no ordinary homicidal maniac. He, or she, as the case may prove, is a dedicated socialist whose mission is the execution of the wealthy bourgeoisie, only occasionally killing a member of the working class who may have become a witness.

FATHER. May God help us.

MISS HASTINGS. This could ruin us. Imagine what the society pages would print about us!

CLURROT. Rather the obituary page you should be worried about.

MISS HASTINGS. How's that?

CLURROT. It would be your passenger list. But be comforted, Miss Hastings, for you have the greatest mind in criminal investigation on the case.

MISS HASTINGS. (*excited*) We do? (*looking out at the audience*)

FATHER. (*excited*) Where? (*looking out at audience*)

CLURROT. (*indignant*) Right here! Are you blind?

FATHER. Oh, of course.

MISS HASTINGS. Do forgive us, Inspector Clurrot. I was looking for Sherlock Holmes.

CLURROT. A story book amateur.

FATHER. One who, I believe, is more than responsible for the sudden rash of deaths by poison – the lovers executioner.

MISS HASTINGS. Really, Father? But how so?

FATHER. In this past year's series he has revealed that cyanide bears the taste of bitter almonds while arsenic a smell of garlic, thus describing a method of disguising them from the hapless victim.

CLURROT. But likewise describing a means of their detection.

MISS HASTINGS. Surely you don't think that popular culture might inspire the criminal mind?

FATHER. I just heard of a case of a woman who poisoned her husband by brewing arsenic in with their afternoon tea. The wife lived because she had been consuming small doses of the poison she had boiled out of fly paper for several weeks, and thus had built up a barely adequate immunity. When on trial she confessed she had gotten the idea from a shilling shocker of short stories. Those rags should be banned.

CLURROT. By the same token, you would be banning Romeo and Juliet. No Father, one should not dispose of the messenger just because one dislikes the message. But I am afraid our discussion of ethics must be postponed for lose on board this ship there is a murdreu.

MISS HASTINGS. Murdreu?

FATHER. Murdreu?

CLURROT. Qui, Murdreu!

> (**MISS HASTINGS** *and* **FATHER** *look at each other, confused. Irritated,* **CLURROT** *grabs the poison and the knife from the trunk and mimes stabbing and pouring.* **FATHER & HASTINGS** *start playing charades.*)

FATHER. A maitre d'?

> (**CLURROT**, *annoyed, drops the knife on the bottle.*)

MISS HASTINGS. A musician!

> (**CLURROT** *grabs the gun and points it at them. They duck.*)

CLURROT. A killer!

MISS HASTING & FATHER. A Murderer!

CLURROT. That's what I said!

FATHER. No you didn't. You said a –

CLURROT. I do not have time for your silly games. There is work to be done, for it is my intention to catch this fiend before the night is through.

MISS HASTINGS. Good show, Inspector.

CLURROT. It would be of great serve, Madam Hastings, if you would keep the passengers gathered here in the dining room. I shall take the opportunity to search their cabins.

> (*He turns to leave.*)

MISS HASTINGS. But Inspector, that doesn't sound quite proper.

CLURROT. Perhaps not. But neither is murder.

MISS HASTINGS. Ah, good point.

FATHER. God's speed.

> (*She smiles her consent as* **CLURROT** *exits, passing* **LORD BENNET** *entering.*)

MISS HASTINGS. Oh, Inspector, what about this (*motioning to trunk, then seeing* **BENNET**) Lord Bennet, I do hope you have found everything so far to your liking?

BENNET. Quite, Miss Hastings, except this blasted fever. The HMS Victoria makes the perfect vessel of matrimony.

MISS HASTINGS. (*flirtatious*) Oh, you're such a wit, Lord Bennet. But you really seem to need someone to take care of you. Should I pop over to the ship's nurse –

BENNET. No, no. I have my own medicine. Carry it with me everywhere.

(**BENNET** *pulls out a bottle of "Fowler's Solution," drinks a sip and puts it down.* **FATHER** *looks over the items on the trunk – putting all back in.*)

MISS HASTINGS. Fowlers? Is that the best for fever?

BENNET. The most powerful.

MISS HASTINGS. Like the men that use it.

BENNET. And my bank holds the overdue note on the company, so I get it free.

MISS HASTINGS. Of course. We are quite flattered that of all places, the Contessa selected our ship for this happy occasion.

BENNET. My bank holds the overdue note on this ship as well.

(**MISS HASTINGS** *nods disappointedly.* **NICOLE**, *in a worn, poorly fitting wedding dress, storms in carrying gladiolus.*)

NICOLE. (*outraged*) Gladiolas? Gladiolas?

(**FATHER** *turns around, smiling at the flowers.*)

FATHER. They're beautiful.

BENNET. Nicole, dear? Isn't it bad luck to be seen before the wedding?

MISS HASTINGS. Perhaps the Father and I should go over the schedule of the ceremony?

(**MISS HASTINGS** *and* **FATHER** *exit.*)

NICOLE. (*pushing the flowers on him*) Don't you know what they say about gladiolus?

BENNET. Actually, no. What do they say about –

NICOLE. (*even more mad*) And look at this dress! I'm a Contessa.

BENNET. It was your mother's dress. She was a touring American vaudeville "artiste," if my memory serves me correctly.

NICOLE. Arthur, how do you expect me, the daughter of the Count Follette, to get married with funeral flowers and in a used wedding dress?

BENNET. I expect you'll do just fine, as you always have. Don't you think white on you is a bit of a stretch?

NICOLE. If I wasn't a lady –

BENNET. You're not.

NICOLE. Alright then.

(*She punches him in the face.* **BENNET** *staggers back into the trunk and rubs his face as* **NICOLE** *straightens her dress.* **BENNET** *begins to peek into the trunk and is interested in its contents.*)

NICOLE. Lord Arthur Bennet, one of the wealthiest bankers of England, rents out the luxurious HMS Victoria for his dear friend's wedding, but won't shell out a few extra francs for a fitting wedding dress? Always a banker.

(**BENNET** *straightens up and moves away from the trunk.*)

BENNET. That's right. Never throw good money after bad. I'm no bloody fool either. At least not anymore.

NICOLE. You're as much of a fool as I am if I go through with this.

(**BENNET** *takes a firm hold of her chin.*)

BENNET. You better go through with it, my little lovely. Otherwise it's Newgate for the both of us.

(*She puts her hand lightly on his hand, which is gripping her chin.*)

NICOLE. I remember when your touch was soft and gentle. When it sent an erotic tingle through my entire body.

When your hands betrayed your innermost desires.

(*She looks deep into his eyes.*)

Is that really all gone?

(*He pulls his hand away.*)

BENNET. Squandered, with the bank's money.

NICOLE. It wasn't squandered, it was loaned out, as banks are prone to do.

BENNET. But the loans were to you until I discovered you're a fake.

NICOLE. I beg your pardon. I am Contessa Follette. My father was Count Follette and his father before him.

BENNET. And the Follettes lost all but their title over forty years ago when their land was overrun during the Franco-Prussian war. You're as poor as a peasant.

NICOLE. A peasant with a title. And titles open a lot of doors, besides making good collateral.

BENNET. How could I have been such a dolt?

NICOLE. You're not the first banker to issue a bad loan.

BENNET. Five bad loans, at a hundred thousand pounds apiece.

NICOLE. Maybe you're the first for that much. Why don't you marry me?

BENNET. What? You're a swindler.

NICOLE. But we were so very happy and there's such a little difference between a banker and a swindler.

(*She moves closer to him. He backs away.*)

BENNET. You're marrying this Rothchild chap and then he's repaying your loans.

NICOLE. He is a playful American boy who's grown up with too much money and too little culture. I don't want to marry him.

(**BENNET** *walks to a male guest.*)

BENNET. You have to. Besides, your father's come all this way from wherever it is he's come from to be here.

NICOLE. My father? But he's dead.

BENNET. May I present Count Follette.

(**BENNET** *has the guest selected to pose as her father stand up. [He should be either the wrong age or nationality.]* **NICOLE** *is shocked.*)

NICOLE. Are you crazy? (*To guest/father*) Nothing personal.

BENNET. Okay, we'll say he's your adopted father. Now get out of here before the lucky groom sees you. We can't have him getting cold feet.

NICOLE. (*to guest/father*) Isn't it touching how he looks out for your daughter? (*to* **BENNET**) I still don't see why we don't just sail right back to the continent – with one last loan from your bank.

BENNET. Because, Nicole dear, sooner or later, there's always a price to pay. If you ruin my life, I'll end yours.

(**JOHN** *and* **VIVIAN** *enter.*)

BENNET. Ah, the Rothchilds.

VIVIAN. Lord Bennet. A pleasure to see you again.

JOHN. Hello, Nicole.

NICOLE. Hi, Johnny.

(**JOHN** *and* **NICOLE** *kiss – a long kiss.* **VIVIAN** *and* **BENNET** *look on. They start to talk as the kiss continues.*)

BENNET. How was your tour of the continent?

VIVIAN. Excellent. Thank you so much for loaning us that Mercedes to putter around in. It was just a dream. I'm so sorry we smashed it up in Luxembourg. I'll buy you a replacement.

(**VIVIAN** *gets out a checkbook.*)

VIVIAN. How much would that be in American dollars?

BENNET. Oh, please, Miss Rothchild. Put your checkbook away. You Americans are much to eager to part with your money.

VIVIAN. Well, I guess it's like my grandpappy always said. Money is like manure. It should be spread around in order to encourage things to grow. Our grandpappy was a farmer back in Oklahoma.

BENNET. Well, in the civilized banking community, we invest rather than spend. As a matter of fact, I could let you in on some rather strikingly fine opportunities.

VIVIAN. I'll try anything once, Lord B. You don't mind if I call you Lord B, do you? It's more informal.

BENNET. (*taking her arm*) How about if we try Arthur.

(*He starts to lead her off.*)

VIVIAN. Arthur? I like that. It sounds so British, don't you think?

(*They exit.* JOHN *and* NICOLE*'s kiss finally comes to an end.*)

JOHN. Scared?

NICOLE. Terrified. You?

JOHN. Shaking like a little boy about to ride his first horse.

NICOLE. That makes me sound like a thoroughbred.

JOHN. Sorry. But to me you are. You sure you want to go through with this?

NICOLE. No. But I'm never sure of anything. I'll do whatever you want.

JOHN. I just want you to boast that beautiful smile and reprise your melodic laugh all day, every day.

NICOLE. Why'd you have to be so sweet?

JOHN. To try to match you.

(NICOLE *steps away from* JOHN.)

NICOLE. John. Would it make any difference if I were –

(ISABELLA *enters, in waitress attire.*)

ISABELLA. Pardon me, madam, sir. But Mr. Rothchild is wanted on the deck by his sister to discuss a slight problem in the wedding arrangements.

JOHN & NICOLE. Problem.

JOHN. Don't fret, my dear Nicole. I'll take care of everything for you from now on.

(**JOHN** *exits.*)

ISABELLA. Follette? That sounds so familiar. Where have I heard that name before?

NICOLE. France?

ISABELLA. Very funny. I know we have met before.

NICOLE. Oh, I'm sure not. I am a Contessa, not a waitress.

(**ISABELLA** *snaps her fingers, remembering.*)

ISABELLA. You remind me of a girl I worked with in Monaco about a year ago, at a small cafe along the Riviera where rich Englishmen would watch the bathing suits wiggle past.

NICOLE. Really? Well, I hope that's a compliment. If you'll excuse me?

ISABELLA. She waited on them at tables and got extra tips for extra service in the boudoir.

NICOLE. Well, then I guess it's not a compliment. Don't you think there's something in the kitchen you should be doing?

(**ISABELLA** *starts to leave.*)

ISABELLA. It is important for even contessas to remember who their friends are. No?

(**ISABELLA** *exits as* **VIVIAN** *enters.*)

NICOLE. (*Straightening up*) Ah, Vivian. Have you seen Lord Bennet?

VIVIAN. Lord B was out on the deck getting some fresh air the last I saw him. Sharing his first course with the fish, if you know what I mean.

NICOLE. Thank you.

(**NICOLE** *exits quickly.* **VIVIAN** *peeks inside the steamer trunk.*)

VIVIAN. (*To herself*) And it couldn't have happened to a more pompous twit.

(**VIVIAN** *finds the contents of the trunk very interesting.* **JOHN** *enters, holding an open ring box.*)

JOHN. (*Angry*) What are these? VIVIAN? What are these?

(**VIVIAN** *quickly straightens up. He hands her the rings.*)

VIVIAN. Let me guess – wedding rings?

JOHN. They're brass.

VIVIAN. (*Moving to a female guest*) Oh, John. You're so worked up, you didn't even notice Mother managed to get here after all those problems with customs.

JOHN. Mother?

VIVIAN. (*To guest/mother*) Aren't men funny when they're all nervous. Why, he's so flustered he hardly even recognized you.

JOHN. Mother? (*To* **VIVIAN**) Are you nuts? – (*to guest mother*) Nothing personal.

VIVIAN. She's the best we can do with what little cash we have left from selling that Mercedes. We'll say she's our stepmother.

JOHN. Has Dad shown up too?

VIVIAN. Now that's a silly question. Of course not. You know he and our stepmother can't stand to be in the same room together since the divorce.

JOHN. Silly me. Mom, maybe you can talk some sense into your daughter here – and give her some tips on picking the appropriate attire. After all, I am her only brother and – (to **VIVIAN**) I am your only brother aren't I?

VIVIAN. (*to guest/mother*) Isn't he a darling? (*to* **JOHN**) Of course you are. Now, just relax, John. After all, this isn't exactly your first wedding.

JOHN. No, but it's the first time she's less than twice my age. Don't you think she might notice these rings aren't exactly gold?

VIVIAN. In the heat of the moment, there'll probably be tears in her eyes.

JOHN. Later it'll be tears in her heart.

VIVIAN. Later it'll be too late. You better not be thinking of backing out on me again, like down in Corsica. Almost had that rich British matron dancing up to the alter when you up and confessed you weren't a Rockefeller but a two-bit gigolo.

JOHN. She was a sweet woman. And I'm an actor.

VIVIAN. You were a flop as an actor. You're a success as a gigolo, thanks to me.

JOHN. Yes, you. The bandit from Oklahoma who tried holding up a small bank in Verona by shouting (*Fake Italian accent*) "Give-a mea your moniesa."

VIVIAN. Well, that's how all the Italians talked back in the States.

JOHN. How could I ever have been fool enough to go along with you?

VIVIAN. When you're desperate enough, you're fool enough to do just about anything. And you were desperate. If I hadn't taken you on you'd still be wandering the streets in a white sheet.

JOHN. I was performing a monologue from Julius Caesar. "Friends, Romans, Countrymen, lend me – "

VIVIAN. – A buck.

JOHN. And how could you be so stupid as to go to a foreign country to hold up banks and not even learn the language?

(**VIVIAN** *pulls out a gun and places it down on the head table.*)

VIVIAN. This speaks every language.

JOHN. (*Looking around, panicked*) What are you carrying that thing around with you for?

(**JOHN** *throws a napkin over the gun.* **VIVIAN** *gives a short laugh.*)

VIVIAN. To make sure you go through with it this time. And if we want to point fingers at stupid, you get all ten pointed at you for deciding to go to France and perform Moriarity on the street.

JOHN. That's Moliere. He was a famous French playwright who traveled the country performing from the back of a wagon. Moriarity is the villain in the Sherlock Holmes stories.

VIVIAN. I knew he was an alright guy.

JOHN. This isn't how I imagined I'd be making a living. Marrying rich women of social standing and then you tell them I'm a gigolo so they'll pay me off to die while on an expedition down the Congo. I have five widows throughout Europe and I've never even been to Africa.

VIVIAN. (*Taking rings from him*) We'll go to Morocco next.

JOHN. This is cruel. And Nicole is such a sweet girl.

VIVIAN. You want out? Okay, but after this wedding at sea. There's talk about a war with Austria-Hungary, wherever that is. You can go off and join the French Foreign Legion. But you lost me a half a million back in Verona.

JOHN. Oh, come on. That was a small bank.

VIVIAN. I'd been watching that bank and it did great business with the upper crust. It was just sitting there in an open vault waiting to be taken. I had just pulled my piece when you walked in shouting "Friends, Romans, Countrymen."

JOHN. And if I hadn't convinced them you were part of my act you'd be in a "prisonna" right now.

VIVIAN. You owe me, Pretty Face. And if this gal is buddy-buddy with Lord Banker then she's got money dripping from her perfumed pores. Now I'm going to ditch these rings with your best man. Go get a stiff drink and think about what you want to do.

(*She leaves, going to the guest selected to play the best man.* **JOHN** *looks curiously at the trunk and begins to look inside, when* **HOWARD** *enters and deliberately bumps into him.*)

HOWARD. Excuse me, sir.

JOHN. That's alright, my fine fellow. Just make sure it doesn't happen again.

(**JOHN** *turns away.* **HOWARD** *is annoyed and bumps into him again.*)

JOHN. Are you doing that on purpose?

HOWARD. Who? Me? The ship lurched.

(**JOHN** *begins to walk away.*)

HOWARD. Stan Meyerhoff.

(**JOHN** *stops dead in his tracks. He then turns around to* **HOWARD**.)

JOHN. Pardon?

HOWARD. You remind me a lot of someone I knew back in the States. A Stan Meyerhoff.

JOHN. Really? Well, I hope that's a compliment.

HOWARD. He was one of the worst actors I've ever bombed in a show with. And I've bombed a lot.

JOHN. Well, then I guess it's not a compliment. Aren't you one of the waiters?

HOWARD. Howard Krepps' the name. I was with this vaudeville show that had its manager run away with the money in Dover, so I landed a job on this ship.

(*They shake hands.*)

JOHN. John Rothchild, of the Rothchilds.

HOWARD. You wish. At least your acting's improved. You know what they say in show biz?

JOHN. What?

HOWARD. Never forget the little people on your way to the top. They might know something.

(**HOWARD** *winks and goes back into the kitchen as* **VIVIAN** *returns.*)

VIVIAN. You're unarmed. I don't want to catch you again without a drink in your hand.

JOHN. (*Indicating best man*) Who's that? Anyone I should know?

VIVIAN. Your best man.

JOHN. (*to best man*) Don't drop the rings, they'll break. (*to* **VIVIAN**) I can't go through with this.

VIVIAN. You can and you will. Think of it as your farewell performance. And the Contessa looks like a fun one to play a honeymoon with. And you owe me.

JOHN. But –

VIVIAN. (*interrupting*) You're going to have to learn something, Pretty Face. In this world, sooner or later, there's always a price to pay.

(*Music* – **VIVIAN** *sings* **"THERE'S ALWAYS A PRICE TO PAY."**)

VIVIAN.

> LIFE IS DELICIOUS
> A WONDERFUL FEAST
> SO MANY MORSELS TO TRY
> HOW CAN WE POSSIBLY TASTE EVERY TREAT
> WITH SO LITTLE TIME TIL WE DIE
> WE SUCCUMB TO TEMPTATION
> WE SAMPLE IT ALL
> OR AS MUCH AS WE CAN WHILE WE MAY
> AND THEN COMES THE CHECK
> AND THAT'S WHEN WE DISCOVER
>
> THERE'S ALWAYS A PRICE TO PAY
> THERE'S ALWAYS A PRICE TO PAY
> THERE'S NEVER A LUNCH THAT'S FREE
> YOU CAN'T HAVE YOUR CAKE AND THEN EAT IT,
> THEY SAY
> THERE'S ALWAYS A PRICE TO PAY

(**BENNET** *and* **NICOLE** *have entered, in their own conversation.*)

LORD BENNET.

> LIFE'S A CASINO
> WE'RE ALL IN THE GAME
> BOTH SKILL AND LUCK ARE THE SAME
> WATCH THE WHEEL SPIN
> IS IT RED? IS IT BLACK
>
> SO EASY TO MAKE A MISTAKE
> THE RICHES ARE TEMPTING

THE POWER IS THRILLING
OF COURSE WE CONTINUE TO PLAY
AND WHO KNOWS, DEAR LADY, WE MAY WIN IT ALL
BUT THERE'S ALWAYS A PRICE TO PAY

THERE'S ALWAYS A PRICE TO PAY
THERE'S ALWAYS THE CARD YOU DON'T SEE
JUST WHEN YOU'RE FLUSH
THEY MIGHT TAKE IT AWAY
THERE'S ALWAYS A PRICE TO PAY

VIVIAN.

LIFE IS PERPLEXING
A PUZZLING MAZE
WHICH IS THE PATH WE SHOULD CHOOSE
SO MUCH TO WISH FOR AMD SO MUCH TO WANT
SO MUCH TO WIN AND TO LOSE

LORD BENNET.

IF NOTHING IS VENTURED THAN NOTHING IS
GAINED
SO YOU MUST LIVE YOUR LIFE FOR TODAY
OF COURSE WHEN TOMORROW COMES CALLING ON
YOU
THERE'S ALWAYS A PRICE TO PAY

(**ISABELLA & HOWARD** *enter separately, off to the
sides.*)

VIVIAN & BENNET.

THERE'S ALWAYS A PRICE TO PAY
THERE'S ALWAYS A BILL THAT'S DUE

ISABELLA & HOWARD.

AND SOMEONE WILL COME TO COLLECT IT
SOMEDAY

JOHN & NICOLE.

THERE'S ALWAYS A PRICE TO PAY

VIVIAN, BENNET, ISABELLA & HOWARD.

THERE'S ALWAYS A PRICE TO PAY
YOUR PAST WILL CATCH UP TO YOU
YOU MAY RUN, YOU MAY HIDE
BUT YOU CAN'T GET AWAY

VIVIAN & BENNET.
THERE'S ALWAYS A PRICE
ISABELLA & HOWARD.
ALWAYS A PRICE
ALL.
ALWAYS A PRICE TO PAY

(*When the song is over* **JOHN** *points out* **HOWARD** *to* **VIVIAN** *and whispers something as they exit.* **NICOLE** *points out* **ISABELLA** *to* **BENNET**. *He sends her out and then intercepts* **ISABELLA** *as everyone else exits.*)

BENNET. Excuse me, miss.

ISABELLA. Is there something I can do for you, sir?

BENNET. Oh, I'm sure there is. What might be your name?

ISABELLA. Isabella Coranova, sir.

BENNET. Isabella. What a lovely name. Quite fitting for the likes of you.

ISABELLA. Oh, sir, you flatter me.

BENNET. You wouldn't hold anything against British bankers would you?

ISABELLA. (*sexy*) I might be tempted to.

(*He takes her hand and looks at it.*)

BENNET. Such a pity to waste such soft hands on such hard work. No ring.

ISABELLA. Sir's eyesight must be failing him. I have rings.

BENNET. I mean one on the third finger. It's a sign my luck is improving.

ISABELLA. Possibly, sir. When you're finished with my hand, it's needed elsewhere.

BENNET. You might be in for quite a wait. I think our hands have taken to each other. It would be a shame to break them up when they're having so much fun. How about we give them a little more time together?

ISABELLA. And what would you suggest we do in the meantime, sir?

BENNET. Oh, I'm sure we can think of something. – I think you have something in the corner of your eye.

(*He moves in close and looks at her eyes.*)

ISABELLA. What is it?

BENNET. Let me look.

(*She lets him look. She's a little concerned.*)

ISABELLA. See anything, sir?

BENNET. Yes.

ISABELLA. What?

BENNET. A speck of vivaciousness.

(*He kisses her. When the kiss ends, she pulls away as if mad, but she hasn't let go of his hand. She gives his hand a forceful tug and leads him off. They exit as **HOWARD** enters, followed by **VIVIAN**.*)

VIVIAN. Excuse me, steward?

HOWARD. Yes, madam? Can I be of service?

VIVIAN. (*sexy*) I'm sure you can.

(**HOWARD** *smiles.*)

VIVIAN. Is it true what they say about shipboard romances?

HOWARD. I'm not sure, Madam. What is it they say?

VIVIAN. That they're like a typhoon, short but just as wet and forceful.

(**HOWARD** *takes her right hand.*)

HOWARD. My lucky day, you're not even a married one.

VIVIAN. You're looking at the wrong hand. The wedding ring goes on the left.

HOWARD. Oh.

(*She shows him her other hand.*)

VIVIAN. But that one's clean too. Not that it matters much to someone like you.

HOWARD. Or you. You have wonderful hands, madam. I bet you're very talented with them.

VIVIAN. So I've been told. I bet you're talented with yours, too.

HOWARD. I'll be happy to give you a demonstration, right after the serving of the next course.

VIVIAN. You'll be my entree. (*She growls at him*)

(*Lights down. The next course is served. During this pause,* **VIVIAN** *takes the bottle of Fowlers Solution and hides it, unnoticed.*)

Scene II

(*Wedding music starts.* **FATHER** *comes out with his prayer book, opens it, pulls a bottle out and takes a swig, then puts it back in.*

JOHN *enters and gets the best man to join him up in front of the* **FATHER**. **BENNET** *enters and goes to the bridesmaid and guest/father and have them wait with him.*

VIVIAN *enters. The march starts.* **BENNET** *will escort the bridesmaid down the aisle.* **NICOLE** *will enter and join the guest/father to walk down the aisle. The priest will open his book and begin once everyone is in place.*)

FATHER. Dearly bewildered. We are gathered here today in the eyes of God to honor and pay our last respects to the dearly departed that lies before us.

(**BENNET** *dashes up and changes the pages for* **FATHER**, *to the marriage section.*)

FATHER. Oh! I thought this was a funeral. I like funerals, they're so peaceful and quiet – just a few sobs here and there.

(**BENNET** *goes and stands by one of the entrances.*)

FATHER. So, you two want to get married?

NICOLE & JOHN. (*Hesitantly*) Yes.

FATHER. Sure?

NICOLE & JOHN. (*Loud*) YES!

FATHER. Okay! Okay. Let's see. (*looks in book*) Dearly beloved. We are gathered here today in the eyes of God to honor the sacred sacrament of matrimony. A union, if you will, of two souls – lost and alone – dying or dead, that need a quiet and lasting burial. Yes, a final resting –

(**VIVIAN** *goes up and turns the pages of the book to the wedding section. She then goes and stands by a different entrance.*)

FATHER. Ah, I mean a restful joining of two hearts. A pair who can now face the world as one. A merger to share what life ahead holds. A union to beat the confederates. Yes, my children, no longer must you languish wondering what you'll be doing Friday night and with whom. Together you will conquer life's challenges and challenge life's conquests. From this day forward, you two shall be one and each of you shall be two – making yourselves five, and marriage is the fifth holy sacrament. Not a sacrament to be entered into lightly, like some of those other sacraments. No, my friends. This is as serious as death. And death, as we all know, is the moment of our final judgement and lasting –

(**BENNET** *makes a loud coughing sound from the back of the house.* **FATHER** *notices* **BENNET***'s stern glare and changes the tone of his sermon.*)

FATHER. – Marriage is a lasting state, one of the original thirteen and without a doubt a state of the union. Who gives this woman?

(*If the guest/father doesn't speak,* **NICOLE** *will nudge him.*)

GUEST FATHER. I do.

FATHER. How quickly our children grow – as if to catch up with ourselves. Do you, Nicole Follette, take this man to be your lawfully wedded husband, in sickness or in health, richer or poorer, for all the days of your lives, til the edge of night, as you have one life to live as this world turns and til death do you part?

NICOLE. (*A little confused*) I do.

FATHER. And do you, John Rothchild, take this woman to be your lawfully wedded wife, to cherish and to hold, to honor and respect, though young and restless, being her guiding light, for generations, as you search for tomorrow, til death do you part?

JOHN. (*A little confused*) I do.

FATHER. Who has the rings?

(*The best man will open the box. If not,* **JOHN** *will nudge him.*)

FATHER. Will you both now pick up one ring.

(**NICOLE** *and* **JOHN** *do.*)

FATHER. Now, while slipping the ring on your beloved's left ring finger recite after me – With this ring I thee wed.

(*Both* **NICOLE** *and* **JOHN** *repeat "With this ring I thee wed," as they both have problems slipping the ring on each other's fingers with only one hand.*)

FATHER. Aptly done. Now, if anyone can think of any reason why these two people should not be joined, let them speak now or forever hold their peace.

(**ISABELLA** *comes hopping in through the door* **BENNET** *stands by. She is bound in rope and spitting the gag from her mouth.*)

ISABELLA. I do –

(**BENNET** *trips her. She crashes to the floor. There is an awkward moment as* **BENNET** *drags* **ISABELLA** *out the door she came through.*)

NICOLE. You were saying, Father?

FATHER. (*A little confused*) Oh – ah – yes, let's see. If anyone can think of any reason why these two people should not be joined, let them speak now or forever rest in peace.

(**HOWARD** *comes hopping in the door beside* **VIVIAN**. *He is tied in a chair and spitting a gag from his mouth.*)

HOWARD. I do.

(**VIVIAN,** *standing beside the door, hits him over the head with a bottle. He falls back onto the chair he's tied to. There is an awkward moment of silence as* **VIVIAN** *drags him on the chair out the door he came in.*)

JOHN. You were saying, Father?

FATHER. I was saying? Oh – yes. I was saying, if anyone present can think of – perhaps we'd best skip that part!

(*looks in book*) Let's see (*he turns pages*) we did the vows, we did the rings, we did the objections –

(**FATHER** *looks first at where* **HOWARD** *entered and then at where Isabella entered.*)

FATHER. And there were no objections. I guess you both just have to sign this marriage certificate –

(**FATHER** *pulls out a multi-paged document and two pens. He hands the pens to* **NICOLE** *and* **JOHN** *and places the document on top of his sermon book for them to sign.*)

FATHER. And its attached 500,000 pound life insurance and prenuptial agreement amendments.

(**JOHN** *quickly looks over at* **VIVIAN** *as* **NICOLE** *quickly looks over at* **BENNET**. **VIVIAN** *and* **BENNET** *both nod that it's okay to sign.* **NICOLE** *and* **JOHN** *both smile as if nothing was wrong. They both sign.* **FATHER** *turns the page and has them sign again, and then once more.* **FATHER** *then folds up the document and puts it away.*)

FATHER. Now that's out of the way...by the power invested in me by the state of intoxication, and before the witnesses present, I now pronounce you husband and wife. We can now kiss the bride.

(**JOHN** *turns to kiss* **NICOLE**, *but* **FATHER** *kisses her first. The wedding music plays.* **JOHN** *and* **NICOLE** *hold hands and have their guest mother and guest Father join them as they walk from table to table, greeting the audience.* **FATHER** *ushers the best man and bridesmaid back to their seats. Meanwhile* **HOWARD** *enters, angry. He is quickly approached by* **BENNET**.)

BENNET. Say, aren't you the chap that got bashed over the head during the ceremony?

HOWARD. I'll say. Now it's my turn to do some bashing. A guy just tries to make an honest buck and gets led on, tied up and then cracked with a bottle as if he were some new ship. Well, they can't sail me off so quickly. I'm gonna torpedo this little scam.

BENNET. (*Worried*) Scam?

HOWARD. Bet your mother's gold tooth on it. This here groom ain't no catch to anyone but the bunko squad. John Rothchild – that's a laugh. Hah! And my fat Aunt Elma's derriere is a national monument! It's time someone wise up his sap of a bride to the fact that the man she married is a flop of an actor named Stan Meyerhoff.

BENNET. Now just a moment here. Are you're telling me that John Rothchild is really some actor named Stan Meyerhoff?

HOWARD. We bombed together in Baltimore. And you want proof? Why'd the groom's sexy pseudo-sister flash me her curves and then tie me up on a chair in a closet? She said she was kinky, but when she left me alone in the closet, it wasn't too long til I figured she was trying to put me away for the night.

BENNET. (*to himself*) I'm ruined. (*to* **HOWARD**) If you'll pardon me.

(**BENNET** *goes to head table and during the next scene removes a napkin covered gun, unnoticed.* **ISABELLA** *enters, mad, and is quickly approached by* **VIVIAN**.)

VIVIAN. Say, didn't I see you take a fall during the ceremony?

ISABELLA. Yes, but now someone else is going to take a bigger fall. I'm going to expose this whole charade.

VIVIAN. Charade?

ISABELLA. Bet the Pope's pinkie ring on it. This here bride is no catch to anybody. Contessa Nicole Follette – that's a laugh! Hah! It's time someone set the story straight for this poor sap of a groom.

VIVIAN. Are you trying to tell me that Nicole Follette isn't really a Contessa?

ISABELLA. Maybe she is, but she was waiting boudoirs more than tables when I worked with her at the same cafe on the French Riviera two years ago.

VIVIAN. Are you sure this is the same Nicole Follette?

ISABELLA. Absolutely. To shut me up this Lord Bull turned on the charm and tied me up in a cabin! I thought he was just getting kinky, but when he left me in the room with my clothes still on – I knew what he was up to.

VIVIAN. (*to herself*) No wonder it was all so easy. (*to* **ISABELLA**) Well, it all goes to show, you never really know what you're getting yourself into, no matter how much you plan. If you'll excuse me.

(**VIVIAN** *walks away in thought. By now* **FATHER**, **NICOLE** *and* **JOHN** *have come back to the head table, where a wedding cake is.* **VIVIAN** *enters with two drinks. She hands one to* **NICOLE**.)

VIVIAN. Nikki, you don't mind if I call you Nikki now, do you, dear?

NICOLE. No, go right ahead.

VIVIAN. John and I have been as close as brother and sister – which we are. So I'd like to propose a toast to our becoming like Sisters.

(**ISABELLA** *comes up behind them.*)

ISABELLA. Mr. Rothchild, I have an important message for you.

FATHER. Everyone, your attention please. I believe now is when the best man is to make a toast to the newly-weds. (*calling to best man*) Come on – up on your feet. Everyone raise your glass (*noticing* **ISABELLA** *is without a drink*). You don't have a drink, my child. I'd give you mine, but it's against my nature. (*to* **NICOLE** & **JOHN**) Should you be toasting yourself? It doesn't seem quite right.

(**FATHER** *takes* **NICOLE**'s *drink and gives it to* **ISA-BELLA**. **FATHER** *takes* **JOHN**'s *drink for himself. [he's now holding two drinks].*)

FATHER. That's better. Now the toast – with God's speed.

(*The guest/best man makes a toast. Everyone drinks.* **FATHER** *drinks both glasses.* **ISABELLA** *falls over dead,* *into the cake. [Sponge covered with icing?].*)

VIVIAN. Isn't that always the case at these sort of things! Someone nobody remembers inviting gets plastered and does a swan dive into the wedding cake.

FATHER. Perhaps she's dead.

NICOLE/JOHN/BENNET/VIVIAN. DEAD?

JOHN. Naw – She's just passed out.

FATHER. No, no. I'm quite sure she's dead. You know what this means, don't you?

(*Everyone looks worried.*)

FATHER. (*Opening sermon book*) It means we need a funeral service. Yes, yes – a funeral service, with all the trimmings. And mourners. Perhaps some incense – (*looking in book*)

(*Everyone looks at him, realizing that he might be crazy.*)

BENNET. Father, I think I saw some incense back in the other room, along with some Gladiolus.

FATHER. (*His eyes lighting up*) Gladiolus? Exactly the thing for a good wake. Why don't you help me drag her back to the other room where I can get everything all set up.

(**BENNET** *takes one of her arms.*)

BENNET. (*Taking other arm*) Yes, yes – Excellent idea. And then once you have everything laid out, I can bring everyone in.

A wedding and a wake. What more could you ask for?

(*They drag* **ISABELLA** *into a back room and then re-enter.*)

FATHER. And now Ladies and Gentlemen, it's time for the throwing of the bridal bouquet. Would all the single ladies take the floor?

(*Some music is played as* **NICOLE** *comes around and stands facing the head table, with her back to the women* *on the dance floor.* **FATHER** *makes* **VIVIAN** *get up and join the women.* **BENNET**, **JOHN** *and* **FATHER** *are all seated next to each other, directly opposite* **NICOLE**. **VIVIAN** *is close to her.* **HOWARD** *works his way up front as* **NICOLE** *throws the bouquet over her shoulder.* **HOWARD** *catches it. As* **NICOLE** *turns to the side to see who caught the flowers, a gunshot rings out from under the head table.* (**BENNET** *fires the gun and then drops it*). **NICOLE** *faints.* **VIVIAN** *goes to her.*)

VIVIAN. (*Disappointed*) She's just fainted.

(**HOWARD** *falls over dead – holding the flowers on his chest.* **VIVIAN** *dumps a glass of water on* **NICOLE** *and walks away.* **NICOLE** *gets up, picking up the gun from under the table. Shocked, she quickly drops the gun in the cake.* **FATHER** *jumps up.*)

FATHER. Mother of mercy! A double ceremony. (*Holding his hands up over his head*) Thank you Lord!

(*He dashes out from behind the table and drags* **HOWARD'S** *body out of the room as* **MISS HASTINGS** *enters.*)

MISS HASTINGS. What? Another of our waiters nipping the liquor?

VIVIAN. I think it was that last shot that got to him.

MISS HASTINGS. You just can't find good help these days. And we just can't have your guests sitting here with empty plates before them.

(*Lights down. The entree is served. During the serving,* **CLURROT** *enters and he asks if anything unusual has transpired while he was gone. He should visit almost every table.*)

Scene III

(*Music. Lights up.* **CLURROT** *walks up to the cake. Then he smells the drink* **ISABELLA** *was drinking, left beside the cake.* **BENNET & VIVIAN** *approach him.*)

CLURROT. Ah ha. Interessante.

BENNET & VIVIAN. I believe that was my drink.

(*As* **CLURROT** *surrenders the drink, they both reach for it.* **BENNET** *gets it.*)

BENNET. (*to* **VIVIAN**) It would be my pleasure to get you a fresh one.

CLURROT. No, thank you. I am on duty.

VIVIAN. Duty?

CLURROT. Oui. I am Inspector Pierre Clurrot.

BENNET. (*To* **NICOLE**, **JOHN** *and* **VIVIAN**) Who invited him?

(*They shrug.*)

BENNET. Now see here, good man. No one's supposed to have been let on board without an invitation.

CLURROT. (*Showing badge*) This is my invitation, Monsieur. I have tracked down the notorious criminal mastermind le Marque La Mort to this vessel and shall apprehend him before we dock in England.

MISS HASTINGS. Good show, Inspector. Who is he?

CLURROT. He? He could just as well be a she, Madam Hastings. The identity of the Marquis La Mort may be a secret now, but I have my suspicions.

(*He looks at* **BENNET**, *then* **NICOLE**, *then* **JOHN**, *then* **VIVIAN**.)

BENNET. Right! I've never been much impressed by French detectives.

CLURROT. (*Annoyed*) French? I'm not French –

NICOLE. (*To* **BENNET**) He's Belgian.

CLURROT. (*More annoyed*) Luxembourg! I am Inspector Pierre Clurrot of the Luxembourg police and I have never failed when it comes to tracking down a murdreu.

BENNET, VIVIAN, NICOLE & JOHN. A Murdreu?

MISS HASTINGS. Please, not this game again. I did so poorly the last time.

CLURROT. A killer.

NICOLE. If you're not sure if this killer is a man or a woman, how are you going to catch him – her – it?

CLURROT. By the cleus.

ALL. The what?

(*Music* – **CLURROT** *sings* "*CLEU, BY CLEU, BY CLEU*")

CLURROT.
I HOPE YOU WILL BE PATIENT
WITH MY METHODOLOGY
IT'S THE KEY TO UNDERSTANDING
CRIMINAL PSYCHOLOGY
I WILL NOT PUT YOU THROUGH THE –
HOW YOU SAY IT – 3RD DEGREE
BUT I WILL INTERROGATE THE WITNESSES QUITE
THOROUGHLY

AS WE ARE THREE TIMES CONFRONTED
WITH A CORPUS DELICTI
YOU MAY FIND IT WILL BE USEFUL
 TO SECURE YOUR ALIBI
I WILL LOOK FOR FINGERPRINTS
I WILL UNCOVER EVIDENCE
I'LL EXPOSE THE PERPETRATOR WHO COMMITTED
THIS OFFENSE
YOU WILL KNOW BEYOND A REASONABLE DOUBT
WHEN I AM THROUGH
THAT THE ONLY WAY TO SOLVE A CRIME IS
CLUE BY CLUE BY CLUE

I REGRET THIS INCONVENIENCE
BUT I MUST BE PRECISE
THERE'S A KILLER ON THE LOOSE
AND HE HAS MURDERED MORE THAN TWICE

NOW WE ALL HAVE OUR SECRETS
AND I DO NOT WISH TO PRY
BUT I WILL DISCOVER MOTIVE AND MODUS
OPERANDI

THE AUTOPSY REPORT
MAY GIVE ME SOMETHING I CAN USE
WHILE OBSERVING EVERY ONE OF YOU
MAY OFFER FURTHER CLUES
I'LL CONDUCT A BACKGROUND CHECK
AND I WILL FOLLOW EVERY LEAD
AND BEFORE THIS SHIP HAS DOCKED, MY FRIENDS
I PROMISE I'LL SUCCEED
IN PROVING THAT THE MURDERER IS YOU – OR YOU-
OR YOU
AND I'LL DO IT BY PROCEDURE
WHICH IS CLUE BY CLUE BY CLUE.

BENNET. Very eloquent, Inspector. But I'm afraid you'll find us all rather "cleu"less this evening.

CLURROT. I think not, Lord Bennet. I believe someone mentioned something about somebody collapsing sometime after the best man's toast?

(*Everyone is a little confused for a moment.*)

BENNET. Oh, yes – that waitress gal. You know how the serving class can't hold their liquor. Never let the drink help, I mean the help drink. I suspect she's one of those wedding crashers anyway.

CLURROT. A cake crasher as well, no?

VIVIAN. It's terrible, isn't it – someone always gets looped to the gills and makes a scene at these things, don't they?

CLURROT. Exactly why I hate weddings. They bring back bad memories.

MISS HASTINGS. You've been married, Inspector?

CLURROT. No.

(**FATHER** *enters.*)

FATHER. I've never done a burial at sea before. Is everybody ready for the dirge?

MISS HASTINGS. Dirge?

CLURROT. Exactament. You see, Madam Hastings, your waiting staff has not passed out, but passed away. Your waitress has expired with the scent of garlic on her lips. And –

MISS HASTINGS. Garlic? Well, that's strange. The Italian menu's not until tomorrow night.

NICOLE. Maybe it was in the cake.

(*Everyone stares at her.*)

MISS HASTINGS. Certainly not, Contessa. Our pastry chef is Albanian.

CLURROT. Then, perhaps your pastry chef can explain this.

(**CLURROT** *pulls the gun out of the cake.*)

FATHER. A cake ornament?

CLURROT. Correction, Father, it is the ingredient that fed the waiter some lead. (*To* **VIVIAN & JOHN**) That is the American saying, is it not?

VIVIAN. This is terrible.

(**VIVIAN** *crosses herself.* **FATHER** *crosses himself.*)

FATHER. The Lord works in mysterious ways, child. Let us begin. (*Acting quickly*) First – the mourners. (*To audience members*) You look like good mourners. Can you sob a few times?

(*They do.*)

FATHER. (*Quickly*) And criers (*to audience members*) Can you cry?

(*They do. He turns to some other audience members.*)

FATHER. And wailers.

(*They'll wail.*)

FATHER. (*On the verge of tears*) Magnifique!

CLURROT. Pardon, Father. But before we have your ceremony, I would like to ask a few questions of your flock.

(**CLURROT** *moves to the guest/bridesmaid.*)

CLURROT. You look so familiar, Mademoiselle. Have we met before? In Paris perhaps? (*Suddenly coming to him*) Of course, the Follies Brigairre. I hardly recognized you at all with your clothes on. And what would an exotic dancer be doing aboard the private cruise in honor of the wedding of the Contessa Follette?

(*She'll answer that she's the bridesmaid. Even if not –*)

NICOLE. (*Shocked*) My bridesmaid? A Follies girl! How humiliating.

(*She hits* **BENNET** *in the arm.*)

CLURROT. Interessante. Now, if you will amuse me as curiosity forces me to question, who gave the bride away?

FATHER. (*Pointing out guest/father*) The Count Follette – right there.

CLURROT. Ahhh. But, unless my memory serves me incorrect – which is never the case – the Count has been dead for some time, (*to* **NICOLE**) no?

NICOLE. (*Has guest/father stand*) Oh, ah, this is the Viscount Follette – my uncle and adopted father.

CLURROT. (*Shaking hands with guest*) Ah, Oui. But of course. (*referring to* **NICOLE**) Ou' que vous alliez, vous ne verrez jamais une telle beaute'.

(*Wherever you may go, you will never see such beauty*)
(*The guest will not know what* **CLURROT** *said.* **CLUR-ROT** *will notice this and become very suspicious.*)

NICOLE. His emotions have left him speechless.

CLURROT. You mean speak French less – if at all. (**CLURROT** *touches his nose.*) My nose tells me there is something very amiss here. Perhaps you may be able to enlighten me as to who gave the fatal toast?

(*Hopefully they'll point out the best man. Even if not –*)

FATHER. The best man, of course, Inspector. He is right there.

(**FATHER** *points him out.* **CLURROT** *approaches him and is about to ask him a question when he stops and studies the best man's face. He suddenly snaps his fingers*)

CLURROT. Sacre' jour! You are the man who tried to hold up the national bank of Luxembourg! You are a lucky dog that we are between territorial waters – otherwise I would have you in chains. Madam Hastings, you will radio ahead to have Scotland Yard awaiting our arrival. (*back to best man*) Make it easy on yourself, Monsieur, tell us what you know of these two murders and I may be able to use my influence with the magistrate on your behalf. Now, how is it that you became the best man to the wealthy John Rothchild, eh?

VIVIAN. I'm afraid he can't do that, Inspector.

CLURROT. No? Porquoi?

VIVIAN. He is a deaf mute.

(*Everyone looks her, shocked.*)

CLURROT. A deaf mute? Then how did he give the toast?

VIVIAN. It comes and goes. His condition is very volatile.

CLURROT. As volatile as yourself, Mademoiselle Susan Star – a bank robber from America wanted in Milan, Rome and Venice for grand theft!

NICOLE. John Rothchild! You mean that woman is not your sister?

BENNET. He's not John Rothchild either. He's some two-bit out of work American actor.

VIVIAN. And from what I hear the Contessa Follette was making her way in life as a waitress serving more than drinks to horny Englishmen. That is until she conned some cash out of you, I'll bet, Lord Bennet.

JOHN. You're a swindler?

BENNET. As soon as we reach England she's getting an annulment.

CLURROT. (*To* **HASTINGS**) It is amazing how quickly the dirt flies once you begin to do a little prying, Oui?

MISS HASTINGS. This is terrible. Everyone was so happy and it was such a lovely wedding up until now. (*mad at* **CLURROT**) I sincerely hope, Inspector, you do not have this affect on all the weddings you attend. No wonder you don't like them. I daresay, perhaps they don't like you either.

(*She storms away from him. Everyone else turns up their nose at* **CLURROT**, *as if it were all his fault.*)

CLURROT. Why is everyone looking at me? The truth hurts, Oui – but do not condemn the messenger. It is not Rosencrantz and Gildenstern that are dead but a waiter and a waitress on board this vessel and a wealthy international financier by the name of Gerard J. Shepard.

BENNET. Old Shepard?

JOHN. Gerard?

VIVIAN. Jerry?

NICOLE. G J?

(*Everyone looks at each other in shock.*)

CLURROT. It would appear Mr. Shepard was well known.

MISS HASTINGS. Or at least he got around.

BENNET. He was a business acquaintance.

CLURROT. One your bank was quite a bit in debt to, if memory serves me correctly.

JOHN. Funny, he never mentioned that. I just met Gerard last week at the Ritz in Paris. Quite an affable fellow. He took me to his club a few times.

CLURROT. And what club might that be?

NICOLE. The Proudhon club in Paris. That's where I met G J, when I was working there about a year ago.

CLURROT. The Proudhon club? Were either of you not aware that this club was affiliated with the notorious Hell Fire Club of England?

JOHN & NICOLE. The what?

FATHER. A gathering place for wealthy elitists who would subvert the cause of syndicalism and anarchy for their own benefit.

JOHN. Well, I never listened to their political discussions. Just sampled the free wine.

CLURROT. And free women? That is also what the Hell Fire Club has a reputation for. (*to* **NICOLE**) No, Mademoiselle?

NICOLE. I was just a waitress.

CLURROT. (*To* **VIVIAN**) And you, Mademoiselle?

VIVIAN. Well, certainly I was never at his club nor am I ever free. I only just met Gerry at the Ritz hotel. He thought he was lucky with cards and women. I'm afraid I proved him wrong – at both.

CLURROT. This recent development may, perhaps, shed a ray of light into the tunnel of suspicion, or merely provide a denser fog.

(*Everyone stares at him, confused.*)

ALL. Pardon?

FATHER. Well, at least we have enough friends present for a proper wake.

CLURROT. Friends? Someone here has proved to be quite the opposite. It would appear that the channel is not the only one being crossed this evening.

VIVIAN. I'll say. Only a British banker would think of finding a rich American to marry off some two-bit tramp he's already had his fill of, as a way to bail him out of some failed financial deals.

NICOLE. Well, you're the pot calling the kettle black. A swindler and inept bank robber. What, did you steal that yacht we had the engagement party on?

VIVIAN. Of course. And I'm still out the francs for that dinner party you two stuffed your faces on. I should bill you for that Lord Bull.

BENNET. I'm ruined. And after spending all that money on renting that villa on the Riviera. And – what really happened to my Rolls?

VIVIAN. We sold it.

JOHN. I'm sorry, Nicole.

BENNET. Sorry! He's sorry! When I have you thrown in prison you'll even be more sorry.

NICOLE. Oh, poor John.

BENNET. What do you mean "poor John?" You're going to prison with him. Inspector, arrest these three at once.

CLURROT. There is a little matter of a few murdreus that I must concentrate my efforts on, Lord Bennet. (*to guests*) Perhaps your kind assistance shall aid us in the search of justice. The deceased waitress-

MISS HASTINGS. Isabella.

CLURROT. Quite – Isabella. Did anyone observe Isabella in conversation with a member of the wedding party? With the Contessa, Lord Bennet or Mademoiselle Rothchild?

(*Audience answers: She knew the Contessa from the Riviera and was blackmailing her. Lord Bennet seduced her. After the wedding Isabella told Vivian the Contessa was a fake.*)

CLURROT. Very interresante, oui. And now the deceased waiter –

MISS HASTINGS. Howard.

CLURROT. Ah, yes, Howard. With whom did he have conversations with this evening? Mr. Rothchild perhaps, mademoiselle Rothchild or even Lord Bennet?

(*Audience answers: He knew John and was blackmailing him. Vivian seduced him. After the wedding he told Lord Bennet John was a fake.*)

CLURROT. There seems to have been quite a lot I missed while searching for our killer in all the wrong places. As the wedding party has revealed themselves to be quite unusual, was the wedding itself unusual in anyway?

(*Audience answers: Father started doing a funeral service. Isabella and Howard appeared tied up, trying to object, but were dragged out again. Bride and Groom signed a long document. Father kissed the bride first.*)

FATHER. Well, Inspector, if you'll not permit us to have our wake, the least you can do is allow us to cut the cake.

(**FATHER** *pulls a large dagger out of the trunk. He takes a hand of* **NICOLE** *and* **JOHN** *and places them on the dagger.*)

FATHER. The bride cuts the cake – the groom cuts the cake –

(**FATHER** *forces them to cut the cake with him, which becomes two stabs to the cake. Meanwhile,* **CLURROT** *has picked up from the head table the marriage certificate and insurance policy and looks it over with great interest.*)

NICOLE. To think, I fell in love with you and you were just seducing me with a warm heart for cold cash.

JOHN. And how blind I was not to see you were stooping so low as to do the same to me.

FATHER. Now, I believe tradition has it that the bride and groom feed each other the cake.

(*They smash the cake into each other's faces.*)

MISS HASTINGS. This is so disappointing. Please, do something, Inspector.

CLURROT. I assure you, I have done all that needs to be done. For I now know the answers to all the missing pieces of this fatal puzzle. Oui, in just a few moments, Madam Hastings, everyone will get their just desserts.

(*Lights down. Dessert is served. Sleuth sheets are collected.*)

Scene IV

(*Music.* **CLURROT** *and everyone else is present.* **FATHER** *has three drinks in front of him.*)

CLURROT. Ladies and Gentlemen, the time has come to arrest the detestable culprit responsible for the murdreus of Isabella Coranova and Howard Krepps.

FATHER. But I never got my chance to –

CLURROT. I am afraid, Father, that we will not be able to have your burial at sea, for Scotland Yard has requested to examine the corpses. In this world today, things are seldom as they appear. Tonight, virtually nothing was what it purported to be. The bridal bouquet was gladiolus, the gold rings were brass, the bride and groom swindlers trying to fleece each other, and all their relatives petty crooks. Perhaps it shouldn't have been too surprising that the reception should turn into a scene of a crime. Both the victims were small-time blackmailers trying to turn this union of two bunco artists into a golden opportunity. But is that enough of a motive for murder? Perhaps. The waitress died with the scent of garlic on her lips. A clear indication of poisoning by arsenic, the main ingredient of Fowlers Solution, which the deceased seems to have drank an overdose of. The waiter was shot with a western American-made gun – found beneath the table by the Contessa, who dropped it in the cake.

MISS HASTINGS. Great Scotch! You mean Lord Bennet poisoned Isabella and Vivian Rothchild shot Howard?

BENNET. I protest my innocence. I left my bottle of Fowlers Solution on the table earlier this evening. Anyone could have taken it.

VIVIAN. And someone snatched my pea shooter after I forgot and left the darn thing on the head table under a napkin.

CLURROT. Exactament. You see, as both of you had discovered the truth about the bride and the groom from their respective blackmailers, the need for a, as the Americans say, dead-men-tell-no-tales solution had evaporated faster then this evening's vows. If neither side of this wedding of impostors had any money, then neither had any to gain. Or did they?

(**CLURROT** *stares them down.*)

CLURROT. After the vows were exchanged, our happy bride and groom signed a marriage certificate, with one very important amendment – a half million pound life insurance policy on each other. A policy someone decided to collect on.

You see, both victims were killed by mistake.

(*Both* **NICOLE** *and* **JOHN** *jump up from their seats.*)

NICOLE & JOHN. You tried to kill me!

JOHN. No –

NICOLE. Never –

CLURROT. Of course not.

(*They embrace and kiss.*)

JOHN. Forgive me?

NICOLE. If you'll forgive me?

MISS HASTINGS. I do so love happy endings.

CLURROT. But the ending has just begun, Madam. Unfortunately, the bride relinquished her drink to Isabella Coranova for the toast, a glass of lethal libation handed to her by her new sister-in-law, Vivian Rothchild. Moments later, the bride stepped out of the line of fire just in time to see Howard Krepps catch both her bouquet and a .22 slug meant for her.

VIVIAN. Which almost got me.

CLURROT. A vengeful trigger finger is not always an accurate one, ne c'est pas, Lord Bennet? As you said earlier this ending to the Contessa, if she lead your life to ruin, you would end hers.

FATHER. You mean I'm in the clear?

CLURROT. For these two, but not the shepherd's pie, Monsieur Marquis La Mort. You gave yourself away when, without a moment of hesitation, you pulled out the very dagger used to kill Monsieur Shepherd from the steamer trunk which I deliberately left sitting out in the open. Oui, you are under arrest.

(**CLURROT** *pulls out a pair of handcuffs.*)

FATHER. A moment please, Inspector. I would like to hazard a last toast to my two homicidally contemporaries.

(**FATHER** *gives one drink to* **VIVIAN** *and one to* **BENNET**.)

FATHER. Thank you for the fun and a couple of good wakes to come.

(**BENNET**, **VIVIAN** *and* **FATHER** *drink.*)

CLURROT. Now that that is out of the way – Lord Bennet, Mademoiselle Rothchild or should I say Star, you are both under house arrest until we reach the shores of England.

(*Both* **BENNET** *and* **VIVIAN** *suddenly choke and fall over dead.* **CLURROT** *quickly turns and glares at* **FATHER**, *who smiles guilty.*)

FATHER. Yes! After all, why should they have all the fun?

LIGHTS OUT.

FIN

PROPS

Newspapers on tables
steamer trunk
check book
two guns
knife
wire
bottle of poison
bottle of Fowlers Solution
gladiolas
two brass rings
service prayer book
insurance policy
ropes (2)
bottle to hit over head
Wedding cake
wine glasses (6)

Also by
David Landau & Nikki Stern...

The Altos

Contempt of Court

Murder at Café Noir

Noir Suspicious

Please visit our website **samuelfrench.com** for complete
descriptions and licensing information